D0536973

Nayberg, Yevgenia,
Anya's secret society /
[2019]
33305247042579
sa   10/28/19

SECRET SOCIETY

Yevgenia Nayberg

To my sons, Anton and Philippe—Y. N.

Copyright © 2019 by Yevgenia Nayberg
All rights reserved, including the right of reproduction in whole or in part in any form.
Charlesbridge and colophon are registered trademarks of Charlesbridge Publishing, Inc.

Published by Charlesbridge
85 Main Street
Watertown, MA 02472
(617) 926-0329
www.charlesbridge.com

Library of Congress Cataloging-in-Publication Data
Names: Nayberg, Yevgenia, author, illustrator.
Title: Anya's secret society / Yevgenia Nayberg.
Description: Watertown, MA: Charlesbridge, [2019] | Summary: Born in Russia,
    where left-handers are frowned upon, Anya learns to use her right hand, except
    when she draws with her imagined secret society of famous artists—then when
    she moves to America, everything is different.
Identifiers: LCCN 2017059678 (print) | LCCN 2017061794 (ebook) |
    ISBN 9781632897091 (ebook) | ISBN 9781632897107 (ebook pdf) |
    ISBN 9781580898300 (reinforced for library use)
Subjects: LCSH: Left- and right-handedness—Juvenile fiction. | Superstition—
    Russia (Federation)—Juvenile fiction. | Drawing—Technique—Juvenile
    fiction. | Artists—Juvenile fiction. | Imagination—Juvenile fiction.
    | CYAC: Left- and right-handedness—Fiction. | Drawing—
    Fiction. | Artists—Fiction.
Classification: LCC PZ7.1.N375 (ebook) | LCC PZ7.1.N375 An 2019
    (print) | DDC [E]—dc23
LC record available at https://lccn.loc.gov/2017059678

Printed in China
(hc) 10 9 8 7 6 5 4 3 2 1

Illustrations done in acrylic on illustration board and digital collage
Display type set in Catalina Avalon Sans by Kimmy Design
Text type set in Constantia by Microsoft Corporation
Color separations by Colourscan Print Co Pte Ltd. Singapore
Printed by 1010 Printing International Limited in Huizhou,
    Guangdong, China
Production supervision by Brian G. Walker
Designed by Diane M. Earley

Anya was born in Russia, in the middle of winter.

When summer came, Anya's mother took
her to play in the park.
    Anya rolled a ball with her left hand.
Again and again.

A blue-haired lady on a bench frowned.
"Your child is left-handed," she said.
The lady shook her head at Anya. In Russia,
doing the right thing meant being like everyone
else. And everyone else was right-handed.

As Anya grew older, she began to draw.
She drew everywhere. She drew all the time.
And she drew only with her left hand.

Soon everyone in Anya's building knew she was
left-handed.

The grandmas in the yard whispered to one
another about it.

One upstairs neighbor told her, "The right hand
is the *right* hand!"

One downstairs neighbor called up to her,
"The left hand is the *wrong* hand!"

When Anya started school, her teacher said, "You cannot use your left hand here. You have to write like everyone else."

Anya tried to write with her right hand.
The letters looked all wrong.

WILL I ever
BE Like
everyone
else?

As time passed, Anya learned to use her right hand. The right hand became a friend. It could cut with scissors. It could write stories. It could hold a spoon.

But the right hand could not draw. Only
the left hand could draw.

The right hand took care of the world around Anya. The left hand took care of the world *inside* Anya. Anything she imagined, the left hand could draw.

But Anya remembered that doing the
right thing meant being like everyone else.
And everyone else was right-handed.

When Anya wasn't drawing, she read. She read about famous artists. She discovered that Leonardo da Vinci was a lefty. Rembrandt was a lefty also. And Michelangelo was just like Anya—he could use his left *and* his right hand.

She figured many people must not know this, or they would think these artists were wrong, too.

Every night, Anya put on her secret mask and
imagined she was drawing in a candlelit workshop.
There, around the table, sat the Great Artists.
They would invite Anya to join them.

All night long they would talk, laugh, and draw.
And they would draw with their left hand.

"This is my secret society!" Anya exclaimed.
"A secret lefty society!"

When Anya's parents told her they were moving to America, she packed her secret mask, her books, and her drawings. She did not want to forget her home. She did not want to forget her secret society.

Anya was excited, but also scared. America
was very, very far away.

Anya's family made a new home in New York City. When she started school, she saw a left-handed desk, a left-handed pair of scissors, and even a left-handed guitar.

To see what would happen, Anya decided to
use her left hand. Her teacher didn't even notice.

In her new building, one upstairs neighbor said nothing when Anya drew with her left hand in the yard.

And one downstairs neighbor said nothing
when Anya sat on the stoop and drew
with her left hand.

Art was everywhere in Anya's new city—inside museums, in parks, and even on subway walls. Art was on the streets and on people's bodies. Artists were everywhere, too. Many artists used their left hand—just like those in her secret society! No one told them their left hand was the wrong hand.

Anya's secret society was no longer a secret.

Growing up in the Soviet Union, I was often told by adults to use my right hand. Russia had always prided itself on tradition, discipline, and conformity. Many countries had abandoned the idea of a "sinister" left hand, but Russia was still holding on. Just as it does in many languages, the word "right" in Russian means correct, which in turn could make "left" seem wrong. Even today in Russia, being left-handed seems unusual.

While lefties were frowned upon, artists were usually admired. Luckily for me, I could draw! Like Anya, I learned to use my right hand very well, but I continued to use my left hand to draw. I could draw well only with my left hand. I wanted to be like everyone else, but more than anything, I wanted to be an artist. My left hand became my special drawing hand.

An artist spends a lot of time in her secret world. It's easy to be happy there. Falling in love with the real world is another story. To do that, sometimes you need to cross the ocean and experience new places and new people. Other times, it's just a matter of growing up.

As I look forward to future creative adventures, I will always have a place in my heart for the secret society of my childhood.